Please Keep Off the Dinosaur

David Henry Wilson was born in London in 1937, and educated at Dulwich College and Pembroke College, Cambridge. He now lectures at the universities of Bristol and Konstanz, West Germany, where he founded the student theatre. His plays have been widely performed in England, America, Germany and Scandinavia, and his children's books – especially the Jeremy James series – have been translated into several languages. His novel *The Coachman Rat* has been acclaimed in England, America and Germany. He is married, with three grown-up children, and lives in Taunton, Somerset.

Please Keep Off the Dinosaur

David Henry Wilson

ILLUSTRATED BY

Axel Scheffler

MACMILLAN
CHILDREN'S BOOKS

First published 1993 by Pan Macmillan Children's Books
Published in paperback 1994 by Pan Macmillan Children's Books

This edition published 1996 by Macmillan Children's Books
a division of Macmillan Publishers Limited
25 Eccleston Place, London SW1W 9NF
Basingstoke and Oxford
www.macmillan.co.uk

Associated companies throughout the world

ISBN 0 330 34571 0

Text copyright © David Henry Wilson 1993, 1996
Illustrations copyright © Axel Scheffler 1996

The right of David Henry Wilson to be identified as the
author of this work has been asserted by her in accordance
with the Copyright, Designs and Patents Act 1988.

5 7 9 8 6 4

A CIP catalogue record for this book is available from
the British Library.

Phototypeset by Intype London Ltd
Printed by Mackays of Chatham PLC, Kent

For Helmut Winter, who started it all

Contents

CHAPTER ONE

Hello, London

'Is London bigger than the High Street?' asked Jeremy James.

'Much bigger,' said Daddy.

'How much bigger?' asked Jeremy James.

'Hugely bigger,' said Daddy. 'It's bigger than the High Street by as much as an elephant is bigger than a piece of cheese.'

Jeremy James gasped. 'Then it must be hugely huge.'

'It is,' said Daddy.

'And it must have lots of toy shops.'

'Hundreds.'

'And lots of sweet shops.'

'Thousands.'

'Can we go to all of them?' asked Jeremy James.

'There are other things in life and London,' said Mummy, 'than toy shops and sweet shops. Now finish your breakfast, or by the time you get to London, it'll be time to come home.'

Jeremy James and Daddy were going to London to see an important lady. ('Is she the Queen, Daddy?'

1

'Well, not quite. She's Mrs Robinson.') They would spend the rest of the day seeing the sights, and would spend the night in a hotel before driving back tomorrow. The name of the hotel, much to Jeremy James's delight, was Hotel Jeremy. Daddy had chosen it specially because, he said, a hotel with a name like that just had to be nice.

Mummy would have liked to go to London, too, but decided that it wouldn't be much fun wheeling the twins around all day.

'Jeffer go Londy,' suggested Jennifer.

'Another time,' said Mummy.

'Kwiffer Londy,' suggested Christopher, hoping it was something to eat.

'Not today,' said Mummy.

She would take them to the park instead. It wasn't so far.

London was a very long way away, and so Daddy wanted to leave as early as possible. Mummy had already packed Jeremy James's bag, and soon he was all ready to go, smartly dressed, hair neatly combed, face freshly washed, and teeth whitely brushed. It took Daddy a little longer to get ready. First he couldn't find some important papers that he was to give to the important lady. Then he couldn't find the important lady's address. When he found the important papers and the important lady's address, he couldn't find his street map of London, and when he'd found the map, he couldn't find the car keys. Daddy was very bad at finding things, though he said

2

this was only because he was so good at losing them. Mummy found the car keys in the medicine cupboard. They should have been in Daddy's jacket, but they weren't. There were some headache pills in Daddy's jacket.

'Shouldn't these have been in the medicine cupboard?' asked Daddy.

Eventually, Jeremy James was strapped into the back seat of the car, and with cheery waves and loud goodbyes, he and Daddy drove off down the street, swung round the corner, and glided slowly and silently to a halt.

'I knew there was something I had to do last night,' said Daddy.

'What was that?' asked Jeremy James.

'Get some petrol,' said Daddy.

Later, Jeremy James and Daddy found themselves in a long grey street with a line of cars ahead of them and a line of cars behind them, and none of the cars were moving.

'Have they all run out of petrol, Daddy?' asked Jeremy James.

'No,' said Daddy, 'they've run out of room. This is London.'

'But if London's bigger than the High Street,' said Jeremy James, 'there should be lots of room.'

'There is,' said Daddy, 'but none of it is where the cars are.'

The cars all moved forward a few feet and then stopped again. The car next to Daddy's was being driven by a bristly man who suddenly got out, waved his fist, and said some words which sounded like some words nobody was supposed to say.

'What's he saying, Daddy?' asked Jeremy James.

'Something like: "Oh dear me, I fear I shall be late",' replied Daddy.

'He didn't say that,' said Jeremy James.

'Well, he may have put in a few worple worples,' said Daddy.

The traffic did eventually get moving, but it wasn't very long before Daddy began to wonder where they were moving to. Somehow the streets of

London seemed to have shifted from where they'd been on the street map. What should have been a left turn must have been a right turn, or what should have been a right turn must have been a left turn, or maybe they shouldn't have turned at all and oh dear it's a one-way street.

As Daddy lefted, righted, scratched his head and worpled, Jeremy James saw something he'd already seen before – which was a little surprising since this was his first trip to London.

'I know that sweet shop!' he cried.

'I expect you do,' said Daddy. 'We passed it five minutes ago.'

At last they turned into a street that was full of houses without any shops, and there Daddy spotted a lady in a uniform. He pulled up beside her.

'Excuse me!' said Daddy.

'You can't stop here,' said the lady.

'I know,' said Daddy. 'But I'm looking for Welbeck Street.'

'You're in it,' said the lady. 'But you can't stop. You're on a double yellow line.'

'Can you tell me where the nearest car park is?' asked Daddy.

'I can,' said the lady, 'but you won't be able to park there.'

'Why not?' asked Daddy.

'It's full,' said the lady.

'Where can I park, then?' asked Daddy.

'Follow any signs that say "Car Park",' said the lady. 'And hope for the best.'

Off they drove again, through streets where there was no parking, past parks with space and no cars, and past car parks with cars and no space.

Finally they came to a flashing sign, Daddy let out a cry of triumph, and they drove down a dark twisting tunnel, past rows and rows of parked cars, and eventually into a space that was just right for Daddy's car.

'Now I know,' said Daddy, 'how Columbus felt when he discovered America.'

They left the car in its special space, left their cases in the car, and walked out into the grey day-light. Jeremy James noticed that the street was full of paper bags, bent tin cans, newspapers and cigarette packets.

'Are we near the rubbish dump?' he asked.

'No,' said Daddy. 'We're in it.'

They now had to find Welbeck Street again. Daddy took out his street map, turned it upside down, looked left, looked right, and looked lost.

'Can I 'elp yer?' asked a shabby little man with a stubbly chin.

'I'm looking for Welbeck Street,' said Daddy.

'Then I can't 'elp yer,' said the shabby little man, and walked on.

By the time a kindly policeman had shown them the way to Welbeck Street, Mrs Robinson – the important lady – had gone to another appointment, but she had left a message: she would meet Daddy and Jeremy James for lunch the next day, if they were still going to be in London.

'Judging by today's experiences,' said Daddy, 'we'll be lucky if we ever get *out* of London.'

CHAPTER TWO

Wax and 20p

After lunch (chicken and chips, ice cream, and Coca-Cola), Daddy said they were very near to a place called Madame Tussaud's, which was full of wax-work figures of famous people. Jeremy James thought it sounded boring, but it had just started to rain, and Daddy said he'd rather be bored and dry than interested and wet.

No sooner were they inside than Daddy seemed already to have lost his way.

'There's a policeman over there,' he said. 'Just go and ask him where the Chamber of Horrors is.'

Jeremy James went up to the policeman.

'Excuse me,' he said.

The policeman looked straight ahead.

'Could you please tell me the way to the Chamber of Horace?'

The policeman told him nothing.

'Excuse me,' said Jeremy James again.

The policeman didn't even excuse him. Daddy came up beside Jeremy James, and started laughing.

9

'He's a waxwork!' said Daddy. 'You're talking to a model!'

Jeremy James stood there amazed, gazing at the model of a policeman which looked just like a *real* policeman. To make sure, he pulled the policeman's jacket, and then touched the policeman's hand. It was cold and hard.

'Was he ever a real policeman?' asked Jeremy James.

'No,' said Daddy. 'Just a lump of wax.'

Madame Tussaud's was full of people who weren't people. It was also full of people who *were* people. And so when they'd looked at some of the people who weren't people, Daddy suggested they should get away from all the people who were people, and go to somewhere that was less crowded.

'What about the Chamber of Horace?' asked Jeremy James.

Daddy said this was full of murderers and witches and gruesome, horrible things that Jeremy James shouldn't see, and so Jeremy James said he wanted to see them. Daddy said they'd give him bad dreams, Jeremy James said he liked having bad dreams, and Daddy said, oh all right then, and it couldn't be worse than driving through London.

In the Chamber of Horrors, some of the people who weren't people had rather nasty faces, but so did some of the people who *were* people. There were also some bloodstained instruments and chopped-off heads and people with bulging eyes and hanging-out

11

tongues. They were just like some of the pictures in Jeremy James's giant book of fairy tales.

'Ug, ugh, yuck, look at that!' gasped Daddy, pointing to a bloodstained woman holding a blood-stained knife over a bloodstained man in a bloodstained bath.

'You shouldn't look at it, Daddy!' said Jeremy James. 'It'll give you bad dreams.'

Daddy had soon had enough of frightening himself, and so he and Jeremy James left Madame Tussaud's to join the thousands of real people out on the streets of London. It was still raining, and Daddy said they would take the underground, which was a railway that was underneath the streets. Jeremy James thought this was another of Daddy's jokes, like the policeman-who-wasn't-a-policeman, but Daddy said it was true, and held Jeremy James's hand as they went down a long, moving, rattling staircase. When they reached the bottom, they walked along a rounded, white-tiled passage in which a straggly-haired young man was playing a guitar and singing in a voice that rattled just like the moving staircase. Daddy gave Jeremy James 20p to drop in the young man's hat, and the young man winked and nodded.

Jeremy James put his hand back in Daddy's, but he was frowning as they walked. An idea was forming in his mind. He waited until they could no longer hear the young man's rattling song, and then he suddenly took his hand out of Daddy's, ran to the

12

white-tiled side of the passage, and sang at the top of his voice:

'London's burning, London's burning. Fetch the engines, fetch the engines. Fire, fire! Fire, fire . . .'

'Jeremy James!' cried Daddy. 'What on earth are you doing?'

'I'm singing,' said Jeremy James.

'I can hear that,' said Daddy. 'What for?'

'So I can get 20p,' said Jeremy James.

Daddy laughed, and so did some of the people who were hurrying by, but nobody gave Jeremy James 20p. Jeremy James wondered why, and Daddy said maybe it was because people in London weren't too keen to hear that London was burning.

13

CHAPTER THREE

The Pigeon Lady

The moving staircase, the 20p singer, and the top of Jeremy James's voice had been whispers compared to the mighty roar of the underground train as it had come out of its tunnel. Like the rest of London it had been full of people, and Jeremy James had found himself nose to knees with a dozen different pairs of legs before at last Daddy said it was time to get off.

It had stopped raining now, and Daddy and Jeremy James walked along a crowded pavement until they came to a huge square. It was elephantly bigger than the market square at home. Cars, buses and lorries roared all round it, there were grand buildings on every side, and towering over it was a very tall pillar on top of which stood the figure of a man. Round the pillar were four stone lions.

'This,' said Daddy, 'is Trafalgar Square. And the man on the pillar is Nelson, who won a great victory for England.'

'Was he a footballer?' asked Jeremy James.

'No,' said Daddy, 'he was a sailor. A great admiral, who won a sea battle against the French.'

'Why did they put him on top of a pillar?' asked Jeremy James.

'As a reward for saving England,' said Daddy.

Jeremy James frowned. Being stuck on a pillar seemed to him more of a punishment than a reward. But it was typical of grown-ups to put Nelson on a pillar when he'd probably have been much happier eating a tub of ice cream and going out to play.

The square was full of people and pigeons. Some of the people were feeding some of the pigeons, and one old lady had them all over her, on her head and arms and shoulders. She was throwing pieces of bread on the ground, or holding them out for the pigeons to come and take, and she was smiling all the time and talking to the birds:

'Come on, my beauties,' she was saying. 'Come an' fill yer tums at Auntie Dot's.'

She caught sight of the wide-eyed Jeremy James.

' 'Ere y'are, sonny,' she said. 'Feed the birds. You be nice ter them, an' they'll be nice ter you.'

Jeremy James looked at Daddy, who smiled and nodded, and the old lady gave him a handful of crumbs.

'Just 'old out yer 'ands an' they'll come,' she said.

And come they did. In no time, a dozen birds had gathered round, on and over Jeremy James. One even landed on his wrist and pecked the crumbs out of his hand. The pigeons were all making a gentle cooing noise, and one sat on Jeremy James's head and sang roocoo, roocoo in his ear.

15

Then Jeremy James felt something warm and soft slipping down the side of his face.

'Oh!' said Daddy.

'Eek!' said Jeremy James.

The something fell with a little plop on to Jeremy James's collar. It was white and sticky.

'What is it?' asked Jeremy James.

'Well,' said Daddy, 'it's normally known as "droppings". But in pigeon English it's sometimes called "Number Coo".'

'That'll bring yer luck, sonny!' said the old lady, and gave Daddy a tissue.

'And what do they do to you if you're unlucky?' asked Daddy.

The old lady laughed.

Daddy tried to wipe Jeremy James's face, but the pigeons were still fluttering all round him. The old lady told him to throw the rest of his crumbs away, and then the pigeons would leave him alone.

'They're jus' like some people,' she said. 'All over yer so long as yer've got somethin' ter give 'em. Not so keen when yer empty-'anded.'

But even when the pigeons had fluttered away, the sticky white stuff still stuck to Jeremy James's collar. The old lady pointed to a fountain across the square.

'A drop o' water's all yer need,' she said. 'Then 'e'll be as clean as a pigeon in a packet o' Persil.'

Daddy took Jeremy James to the fountain, and

17

washed his face and collar till all the sticky white stuff had gone.

'Will I be unlucky now?' asked Jeremy James.

'Not unless someone gives you a loaf of bread,' said Daddy.

They walked back across the square to say good-bye to the old lady, and now Jeremy James saw that she was not only covered with pigeons. She was also covered with 'Number Coo'.

'You must be very, very lucky,' said Jeremy James.

'Oh I am, sonny,' she said, 'I am. Look at all the friends I got, an' the nice people I meet. An' I'll tell yer somethin' else. 'Ave you ever bin on the Underground?'

'Yes,' said Jeremy James.

'An' yer've seen 'ow crowded it is?'

'Yes,' said Jeremy James.

'Well,' said the old lady. 'When I gets on, yer should see 'ow quick the carriage empties. Auntie Dot never 'as no trouble wi' crowds. Except o' course wi' crowds o' pigeons.'

CHAPTER FOUR

The Pry Monster

When they said goodbye to Auntie Dot, Daddy and Jeremy James walked down a broad street which was called Whitehall. Jeremy James wondered if it was called Whitehall because the pigeons had been there as well. In the middle of the street was a large white block which Daddy said was the Cenotaph, and was a monument to people who had been killed in the war.

'Is war a good thing?' asked Jeremy James.

'No,' said Daddy. 'It's very bad.'

'Did Nelson fight a war?'

'Yes, against the French.'

'Well, if war's a bad thing, why did they put Nelson on top of a pillar, if being on top of a pillar is a good thing?'

Daddy explained that war was bad, but winning a war was good. Jeremy James asked if winning a war was good for the people who had been killed, and Daddy said no, and it wasn't even good for the people who hadn't been killed.

'So who *is* it good for?' asked Jeremy James.

'Nobody really,' said Daddy, 'except soldiers and politicians.'

'Who's Polly Tishuns?' asked Jeremy James.

Daddy explained that politicians were people who told other people what to do, and pretended it was for their own good.

'Is Mummy a Polly Tishun?' asked Jeremy James.

'No,' said Daddy. 'When Mummy tells you to do something, it *is* for your own good. And when I tell you to do something, it's also for your own good. But when politicians tell you to do something, it's usually for *their* good.'

By now they had reached a narrow street which was closed off by a gate, and Daddy said this was Downing Street, where the Prime Minister lived. The Prime Minister was the bossiest politician of them all. Even the politicians who told everyone else what to do were themselves told what to do by the Prime Minister. And as a matter of fact, said Daddy, it was the Prime Minister who was ruining the country.

At that moment there was a buzz of excitement from all the people standing near the gate, and everybody moved back as it was opened. Through it came a group of smartly dressed people surrounded by a group of less smartly dressed people who were carrying cameras, microphones, notebooks and pencils.

'Look!' said Daddy. 'It's the Prime Minister!'

Suddenly the whole group stopped, right next to Daddy and Jeremy James, and the Prime Minister –

with a smile that came straight from the mouth – leaned down and asked Jeremy James his name.

'Jeremy James,' said Jeremy James.

'And do you know who I am, Jeremy James?' asked the Prime Minister.

'You're the Pry Monster,' said Jeremy James.

'Prime Minister,' said the Prime Minister. 'Good! What a clever boy. And are you going to vote for me at the next election, eh?'

Jeremy James didn't know what an election was, but the look on the Prime Minister's face made it clear that Jeremy James was supposed to say yes.

'No,' said Jeremy James.

The Prime Minister looked surprised.

'Oh? And may I ask why not?'

'Because,' said Jeremy James, 'you're ruining the country.'

The Prime Minister looked even more surprised. The smile disappeared from his face, and he glanced at the people around him.

'Ahem!' he said. 'He obviously means *running* the country.'

'No I don't,' said Jeremy James. 'You're a bossy Polly Tishun.'

'Ha ha ha!' unlaughed the Prime Minister, glaring at Daddy, who studied the top of Jeremy James's head. 'Another little joke from the Opposition.' And he walked quickly and stiffly away.

A man with a camera took a photograph of

Jeremy James, and another man with a notebook came up to him.

'Well done, young man!' he said. 'We'll have you on the front page tomorrow. "Jeremy James accuses Prime Minister of ruining the country".'

Everybody was smiling and nodding and congratulating Jeremy James. He wasn't quite sure what all the fuss was about, but he had a strange feeling that perhaps one day he might be put on top of a pillar, like Nelson, for having saved England.

CHAPTER FIVE

More Polly Tishuns

Further along the road, Daddy and Jeremy James came to a very grand and beautiful place called the Houses of Parliament, which was where Polly Tishuns met to tell one another what to do.

There was a small queue at one of the doors, and Daddy said they were lucky, because usually it was a large queue.

'I know why we're lucky,' said Jeremy James.

'Why?' asked Daddy.

'Because of the pigeon's "Number Coo",' said Jeremy James.

'Or "Number Queue",' said Daddy. 'Well, whatever it is, it's worked, because we're going in.'

At the entrance a man in uniform was searching people. When it came to Jeremy James's turn, the man looked very seriously at him, and asked if he had any guns or bombs. Jeremy James said he hadn't, but he'd like some if the man was giving them away.

'In this place,' said the man, 'you won't catch *anyone* giving anything away.'

Daddy and Jeremy James walked up stairs and along corridors, all of which were lined with statues and pictures, and then they suddenly found themselves on a sort of balcony. The balcony overlooked a very strange room: it was high and rather dark, and on both sides of a narrow gangway there were rows and rows of mainly empty green seats. A man in a funny wig was sitting at the far end of the room, and in the green seats were about thirty people, half of whom seemed to be asleep. Daddy and Jeremy James sat down to watch.

'It's all the Government's fault!' cried a thin man on one side of the room.

'Oh no it's not!' shouted a fat man on the other side.

'Oh yes it is!' cried the thin man.

'Order!' said the man in the wig. 'Order! Order!'

Jeremy James asked Daddy what was happening, and Daddy explained that this was called a debate. The Polly Tishuns were discussing what the Government had done, was doing, or was going to do: one side would say it was all very good, and the other side would say it was all very bad. At the end of the discussion, the Polly Tishuns would vote, and the side that said it was all very good would win.

'If they know who's going to win,' said Jeremy James, 'then why do they play?'

Daddy said it was all to do with some long word that Jeremy James didn't understand, and Jeremy James thought it was all to do with grown-ups doing silly things like sticking Nelson on a pillar.

Meanwhile, the debate continued:

'The Government,' said the thin man, 'is ruining the country.'

'Hear, hear!' said a bald man near him.

'Nonsense!' shouted the fat man. 'You'd ruin the country if you were in government.'

'Hear, hear!' said a hairy lady near him.

'No we wouldn't!' said the thin man.

'Yes you would!' said the fat man.

'Order!' said the man in the wig. 'Order! Order!'

'Since we are not in government,' continued the thin man, 'and since all the experts agree that the country is being ruined, and since the Government

claims that it is not responsible for ruining the country, then may I ask who is?'

'The Pry Monster!' shouted Jeremy James.

All heads turned, and there was loud laughter and applause from the people on the balcony and the people on the thin man's side of the room. Some of the people on the fat man's side woke up and didn't look very pleased. And on the balcony was a man in uniform who didn't look very pleased either. He started walking towards Jeremy James.

Daddy, with a rather red face, stood up.

'Come on, Jeremy James,' he said. 'Let's go and see the Queen instead.'

He took Jeremy James's hand just as the uniformed man arrived.

'Sorry about that,' said Daddy, 'but we were leaving anyway.'

Daddy and Jeremy James left the balcony, accompanied by the uniformed man and a round of loud applause.

'Sorry,' said Daddy again, when they were out in the corridor.

'That's all right, sir,' whispered the uniformed man. 'Made my day, that has.'

CHAPTER SIX

Seeing the Queen

'Does the Queen really live here?' asked Jeremy James.

'Yes,' said Daddy.

'It's as big as the Houses of Polly Mint.'

'Kings and queens always have big houses.'

'It must take her ages to hoover the carpet,' said Jeremy James.

They were standing outside Buckingham Palace, and Jeremy James gazed up at all the windows and wondered which one the Queen would look out of. Daddy said she might not look out of any of them, because she might not be there.

'If I had a house like that, I'd always be there,' said Jeremy James.

'So would I,' said Daddy. 'I'd never find my way out.'

'What do kings and queens *do*, Daddy?' asked Jeremy James.

'Well,' said Daddy, 'when they're not hoovering the carpet, they travel around meeting people. They open buildings, launch ships, and ride through the streets so that people can cheer them and wave their flags.'

'How do you become a king?'

'The best way is to get yourself a father who's a king. And make sure you haven't got any older brothers.'

'*I* haven't got any older brothers,' said Jeremy James.

'No,' said Daddy. 'But unfortunately, I'm not a king. Which I'm afraid means that you won't be a king either.'

This was a bit of a blow for Jeremy James. He rather liked the idea of being king. He could easily live in a big house like the Queen's, and he was good at meeting people, and he'd be very good at riding through the streets and being cheered. He wasn't sure how to open buildings or launch ships, but maybe somebody else could do that, and he would do some extra meeting people and being cheered.

'Can't *you* become a king, then, Daddy?' he asked.

Daddy shook his head.

'Well, could the Queen make *me* a king, then?' asked Jeremy James.

'You can ask her,' said Daddy, 'if you see her.'

The problem was how to see her. Even if she came to one of the windows, she'd be much too far away for Jeremy James to talk to. He'd need to go into the Palace itself. But when he told Daddy that he wanted to go into the Palace, Daddy said he'd never be allowed in, and it was time they were going anyway.

'They might let me in if I ask nicely,' said Jeremy James.

'I don't think so,' said Daddy, 'but you can try. There's a guard through the gate there. You can ask him, but if he says no, then we'll leave. Right?'

Jeremy James walked along the railings to a gate which was open, and standing inside the gate was a guard in a red uniform, with a high furry hat that came down over his eyes. He was standing very still, holding his gun like a walking stick, and staring straight ahead. Jeremy James went up to him.

'Excuse me,' he said.

The guard didn't move.

'Please can I go and see the Queen?'

Not a movement, not a word, not a blink. The guard was as stiff as a statue.

Suddenly Jeremy James began to laugh. Daddy had played another trick on him. This wasn't a real guard at all. He was a waxwork, like the models in Madame Tussaud's!

Jeremy James pulled the guard's tunic and poked his hand.

'If you don't go away, little boy,' said the guard out of the corner of his mouth, 'you'll get a thick ear.'

Jeremy James leapt back in amazement.

'I thought you were a waxwork,' he said.

'I may look like a waxwork,' said the guard, 'and

sometimes I feel like a waxwork, but I can give you a thick ear like no waxwork has ever given you.'

'I only want to see the Queen,' said Jeremy James.

'Well you can't,' said the guard. 'She's not at home.'

'Will she be back soon?' asked Jeremy James.

'Not till next Thursday,' said the guard. 'Can I give her a message?'

'Could you tell her that I want to be king?'

'Certainly, sir. And who shall I say was calling?'

'Jeremy James,' said Jeremy James.

'All right, Jeremy James, I'll inform Her Majesty,' said the guard. 'Now hop it before you get me into trouble.'

Jeremy James hopped back to Daddy, who was watching from the other side of the railings.

'Well, what did he say?' asked Daddy.

'He said he'd give me a thick ear,' said Jeremy James, 'and he'll tell the Queen I want to be king.'

'That's nice of him,' said Daddy. 'Or half nice of him.'

'But the Queen won't be back till Thursday,' said Jeremy James.

'That's bad luck,' said Daddy. 'We'll be gone by then.'

CHAPTER SEVEN

The Taxi Driver

It was time to leave Buckingham Palace anyway, because Daddy wanted to go to the hotel.

'We'll take a taxi,' he said, 'have a wash and a rest, and then get ready to see London by night. Agreed?'

Jeremy James agreed – except for the bit about a wash. That was another silly grown-up idea. When you got up, you had to have a wash. When you went out, you had to have a wash. When you came home, you had a wash, and when you went to bed you had a wash. Jeremy James reckoned that if he kept on washing whenever he was told to wash, pretty soon he'd finish up with no face left to wash. And then what would they do?

'Look, Mummy and Daddy,' he'd say. 'I haven't got any face.'

'Oh!' they'd say. 'Who are you?'

'Jeremy James,' he'd say.

'Well, Jeremy James,' they'd say, 'go and wash your blank space.'

Washing was a waste of soap, a waste of water, and a waste of face.

Jeremy James and Daddy stood by the roadside, and Daddy waved to a taxi, but the taxi took no notice. Another taxi came, Daddy waved again, and the second taxi took as much notice as the first taxi. A third and fourth taxi also went by, but when Jeremy James helped Daddy to wave at a fifth taxi, the people sitting in it waved back.

'They were nice,' said Jeremy James.

At last an empty taxi drew up beside them, and they climbed in.

'Hotel Jeremy, please,' said Daddy to the taxi driver, who was a thin man with glasses on his nose, stubble on his chin, and a flat cap on his head.

' 'Otel Jeremy?' repeated the taxi driver. 'Never 'eard of it.'

'It's in Jeremy Street,' said Daddy.

'Jeremy Street?' repeated the taxi driver. 'Never 'eard of it.'

'It's very near Welbeck Street,' said Daddy.

'Welbeck Street?' repeated the taxi driver. 'Where's that?'

'Um, well . . .' said Daddy.

'I wish you people'd pick places what I've 'eard of,' grumbled the taxi driver. 'I'm sick o' people goin' ter places I don't know. Makes my job very difficult.'

'Sorry,' said Daddy, 'but I thought that since you're a taxi driver . . .'

'Yeah,' said the taxi driver, 'ev'rybody finks that because yer a taxi driver yer must know everyfink. Where's this place? they ask. Where's that place? 'Ad someone this mornin' ask me the quickest way to 'Ighgate Cemetery. I told 'im the quickest way was ter jump under a bus. Now then . . .'

He pulled out a book, took off his glasses, muttered, 'Welbeck Street, Welbeck Street, Welbeck Street', and began to flick through the pages.

'Welbeck Street,' he said. 'Got it. Wot was the uvver street?'

'Jeremy Street,' said Daddy.

'Jeremy Street, Jeremy Street, Jeremy Street,' said the taxi driver. 'Jeremy Street. Got it. Is that where yer wanter go?'

'Yes, please,' said Daddy.

'Couldn't 'ave picked a much smaller street, could yer? No wonder I've never 'eard of it.'

They set off through the streets of London, and as the taxi dodged in and out of the traffic, the driver kept telling Daddy what terrible drivers all the other drivers were. Daddy said it must be a really difficult job, and the taxi driver said he'd only been doing it for three days, and if the next three days were as bad as the first three days, he wouldn't be doing it for much longer.

'London,' he said, 'is full o' people 'oo don't know where they're goin, an' drivers 'oo don't know wot they're doin'.'

'Daddy never knows where he's going,' said Jeremy James.

'I do know where I'm going,' said Daddy. 'I just don't know how to get there.'

'I got the same problem,' said the taxi driver. 'I dunno 'ow I managed ter pass me taxi-drivin' test, 'cos I ain't got no sense o' direction.'

Daddy asked him what he'd been doing before he became a taxi driver.

'I was a tourist guide,' he said. 'I only 'ad *that* job fer three days an' all. Took a party o' tourists to 'Ampton Court an' lost 'em in the maze.'

Jeremy James asked Daddy what a maze was, and he explained that it was a lot of paths that led into a place you couldn't get out of. Jeremy James asked if London was a maze, and Daddy said it was worse than a maze because it was just as difficult to get in as to get out.

'Not ter mention gettin' 'round,' said the taxi driver, pulling in to the kerb. 'I'm lost.'

He pulled out his book.

'Now, where was it yer wanted ter go?' he asked.

'Daddy!' said Jeremy James. 'Isn't that our car park over there?'

'So it is!' said Daddy.

'Ah!' said the driver. 'Found it, 'ave I?'

'Pretty nearly,' said Daddy. 'This'll do, anyway.'

'Well fancy that!' said the driver. 'Must be my lucky day!'

Daddy and Jeremy James got out, and Daddy paid before they said goodbye to the driver and set off towards the car park. When Jeremy James looked back, the taxi was still there, and the taxi driver had taken off his glasses and was looking at his book.

'Do you think he'll find his way home?' asked Jeremy James.

'No,' said Daddy. 'And do you think we'll find our way to the hotel?'

'No,' said Jeremy James.

But before they didn't find their way to the hotel, Daddy wanted to fetch the cases from the car, and that meant finding the car. This might not have been quite so difficult if Daddy had remembered which floor it was on. Jeremy James remembered that it was in a space between two other cars, but for a long time they couldn't find the space or the other

two cars. And when at last they did find it, Jeremy James realized that the space had been filled. Daddy's car was in it.

They took out their bags, and then Daddy asked the car park attendant the way to Jeremy Street. Fortunately, it was only two minutes' walk away, and so in exactly ten minutes (after Daddy had turned left instead of right) they found themselves outside a tall dark building with a big sign over the door that read: HOTEL JEREMY.

CHAPTER EIGHT

The Bushy Man

Daddy and Jeremy James walked into the hotel. In the hallway a man was sitting at a table with his head in his hands and a bottle and glass next to his right arm.

'Good afternoon,' said Daddy.

The man raised his head, and Jeremy James found himself staring up at a square-shaped face with a bushy moustache and two bushy eyebrows. The two eyebrows were so bushy that at first Jeremy James thought the man had three moustaches.

'What a life!' said the man.

'It's not that bad, is it?' asked Daddy.

'Maybe yours isn't,' said the man. 'Business is terrible.'

'Oh dear,' said Daddy.

'I can't pay my mortgage.'

'Oh dear.'

'The chambermaid left last week.'

'Oh dear, oh dear.'

'And my wife left this morning.'

'Oh dear, oh dear, oh dear.'

'What a life!'

The bushy man poured some drink out of the bottle into the glass, and swallowed it with one gulp.

'I suppose you want a room,' he said.

Daddy explained that he'd already reserved a room by telephone, and the man looked in a book, said 'Ah!', stood up and sat down.

'Room thirty-three,' he said, 'third floor. Key's over there. I'd get it for you, but I'm having difficulty standing up.'

Daddy went behind the table and took a key down from a board that was full of keys.

'Lift's not working,' said the man. 'Nothing works in this hotel, including me. What a life!'

Daddy and Jeremy James made their way to the stairs.

'People aren't very happy in London, are they?' said Jeremy James to Daddy as he stomped upwards.

'Some of them are,' puffed Daddy.

'Well the bushy man isn't,' said Jeremy James. 'And the taxi man wasn't, and the Pry Monster wasn't, and the Polly Tishuns weren't.'

'The pigeon woman was happy,' panted Daddy. 'And we're happy, aren't we?'

'Yes,' said Jeremy James. 'I'm always happy.'

'So there are some happy people in London,' gasped Daddy. 'Though I shall be a lot happier when we've reached the third floor.'

Room 33 was at the end of the corridor. It was

41

a small room with two beds, a chair and a table, a
wardrobe, a wash basin, and . . . a telephone.

'Ah!' said Daddy. 'I'll tell you what we'll do. We'll
have a wash, and then we'll phone Mummy, shall
we?'

'You have a wash, Daddy,' said Jeremy James,
'and I'll phone Mummy.'

Daddy said they should both have a wash, and
both phone Mummy. Jeremy James pointed out that
he'd already had a wash in the fountain, but Daddy
pointed out that they hadn't had any soap. Jeremy
James noticed that there wasn't any soap in the wash
basin, but Daddy took a small packet out of his bag.
Jeremy James thought that was a piece of bad luck,
but Daddy said it was a piece of soap.

When they'd finished washing, Daddy lifted Jeremy James up on to the table beside the telephone, so that they could ring Mummy.

'Would you like to press the numbers?' asked Daddy.

'Yes, please,' said Jeremy James.

Daddy took Jeremy James's hand and pressed his forefinger on the number 0. But before he could press another number, there was a ringing tone.

'What a life!' said a voice at the other end.

'Oh!' said Daddy. 'Is that reception?'

'Of course it's reception,' said the voice. 'What were you expecting, Buckingham Palace?'

'Sorry,' said Daddy, 'but I wanted to ring home.'

'Dial nine for an outside line,' said the voice. 'You might not get it, but it's worth a try.'

Daddy put the phone down, picked it up again, and pressed Jeremy James's finger on to the number 9. There were a few clicks, and then a humming noise.

'We're in luck,' said Daddy.

Jeremy James liked the telephone. It was a funny feeling talking to someone who wasn't there but whose voice came right into your ear. Once, when he'd been alone in the living room, he'd dialled a number and talked to a lady who lived hundreds of miles away. She'd even sent him a present afterwards. Jeremy James thought it was wonderful. Daddy thought it was expensive, and Jeremy James had been forbidden to do any more dialling.

43

It was Mummy who answered the phone, and when Daddy had said hello, he let Jeremy James talk to her.

'Hello,' said Jeremy James.

'Hello, Jeremy James,' said Mummy. 'Are you enjoying London?'

'Yes,' said Jeremy James. 'Everybody's unhappy except Daddy and me.'

'What are they unhappy about?' asked Mummy.

Jeremy James told Mummy all about the bushy Mr What-a-Life, the taxi driver who couldn't find the way, the Pry Monster who was ruining the country . . .

'And a pigeon did a Number Coo on my head,' said Jeremy James.

'Was the pigeon unhappy, too?' asked Mummy.

'Yes,' said Jeremy James, 'because he must have had a tummy ache.'

Jennifer was next on the phone.

'Hello, Jeffer,' said Jeremy James.

'Jem Jem!' said a delighted voice. 'Jem Jem gone Londy.'

'London,' said Jeremy James. 'Are you being a good girl?'

'No,' said Jennifer. 'Jeffer nor-ty.'

'You always are,' said Jeremy James.

Mummy also passed the phone to Christopher. Jeremy James said, 'Hello, Kwiffer,' but Kwiffer didn't say anything. Mummy told him to say something, but he still didn't say anything, and so Mummy asked to talk to Daddy.

After everybody had talked to everybody (except Kwiffer, who wouldn't talk to anybody), Daddy finally put the phone down.

'I like telephones,' said Jeremy James. 'When I grow up, I'm going to telephone a lot.'

'Well when you grow up,' said Daddy, 'just remember – if you want to say a lot, you're going to have to pay a lot.'

That was another grown-up idea: if you wanted something nice, you always had to pay for it. Nasties were free. You could have as many washes as you liked, and you wouldn't have to pay a penny.

'When I'm king,' said Jeremy James, 'nobody will have to pay for telephones.'

And secretly he added that when he was king, soap would cost a fortune.

CHAPTER NINE

An Amazing Meal

After a little rest, Daddy and Jeremy James were ready to see London by night.

'Off to enjoy yourselves, are you?' said the bushy man at the table.

'Yes,' said Jeremy James. 'We're going to be happy.'

'Lucky you,' said the man.

'What are *you* going to do?' asked Jeremy James.

'I'm going to stay here,' said the man, 'and be miserable.'

'You won't be happy if you're mizzable,' said Jeremy James.

'The way I feel,' said the man, 'I wouldn't even be happy if I was happy. What a life!'

It was dark outside now. Soon Daddy and Jeremy James were walking along a street full of brightly lit shops, red double-decker buses, black box-like taxis, hundreds of cars, and thousands of people. This road suddenly broadened out into a roundish area with streets going off at all angles, and huge flashing signs that kept changing their appearance.

'This is Piccadilly Circus,' said Daddy.

'I can't see any circus,' said Jeremy James.

'There isn't one,' said Daddy. 'That's just its name.'

'They shouldn't call it a circus if it isn't a circus,' said Jeremy James. 'That's cheating.'

They walked up one of the streets that led off Piccadilly Uncircus, and it had a lot of theatres in it.

'Would you like to go to the theatre tonight?' asked Daddy.

'Yes, please,' said Jeremy James.

'Right,' said Daddy, 'let's see if we can get two tickets.'

The theatre they went to had a lot of pictures of wolves outside, and Daddy said there was a musical show called *Wolfie* here, which he thought Jeremy James might enjoy. And when he'd bought the tickets, he had another suggestion: 'How about something to eat before the show?'

Daddy was full of good ideas this evening. He even knew which restaurant they would go to, *and* where it was. You had to go along the street, turn right here, and left here, and . . . no, wait a minute, back we go . . . it should have been right here, and left here, and . . . back we go . . . ah! There it is! The restaurant was called Le Campanile which Daddy said was French for bell tower, though it hadn't got a bell and it wasn't in a tower.

They were welcomed by a tiny bald man in a black jacket and bow tie.

47

'Bonsoir, messieurs,' he said. 'You veesh to ev a table for two personnes? Bon, come zees way, pleeze.'

He took them to a table in the corner, fetched a high cushion for Jeremy James, bowed his head to them both, and then with a flourish of his hand produced a menu.

Daddy read through the list, and Jeremy James chose chicken and chips, but Daddy said he'd had chicken and chips for lunch, and wouldn't he like to try something else? Like veal escalope, for instance? Jeremy James had never heard of Willy's gallop, but it did sound quite interesting, and since it came with chips, he said yes, all right.

Willy's gallop proved to be a success: thin slices of meat covered in golden batter, very tender, very tasty. And the chips were just as golden, crisp and crunchy.

'You don't want any dessert after that, do you, Jeremy James?' asked Daddy, when the last golden crumb had disappeared.

'Yes I do!' said Jeremy James.

A meal without a dessert was like Nelson's Column without Nelson.

'Right,' said Daddy. 'Follow me.'

Jeremy James followed Daddy across the restaurant to a large lighted cabinet. On the open shelves of the cabinet stood dish upon dish of puddings, pies, mousses, gâteaux, trifles, tarts, jellies, fruit salads, ice cream . . .

'Help yourself,' said Daddy.

Jeremy James's eyes opened as wide as two dessert bowls.

'To anything?' he asked.

'Whatever you like,' said Daddy.

'As much as I like?' asked Jeremy James.

'As much as you can get in the bowl,' said Daddy.

No dessert bowl was ever piled as high as Jeremy James's. He took a portion of pudding, a piece of pie, a mountain of mousse, a tremble of trifle, a tingle of tart, a judder of jelly, and an iceberg of ice cream. Heads turned to look at the amazing dessert bowl with legs as it made its way carefully across the restaurant to the table in the corner.

'You'll never be able to eat all that,' said Daddy, though his own bowl was almost as high as Jeremy James's.

'Nor will you,' said Jeremy James.

They were both wrong.

For the next ten minutes not a word was spoken, as spoons and forks scooped and sliced and squelched their way through the multi-coloured mouthfuls. If every Londoner could come and have dinner in the bell tower, thought Jeremy James, they would never be unhappy again.

When at last the bowl was empty, and Jeremy James was full, the little bald man in the black jacket and bow tie came to the table.

'Deed you enjoy ze meal?' he asked.

'Yes, thank you,' said Jeremy James. 'It was the best meal I've ever had.'

'Ah bon!' said the man. 'Zen per'eps you weel come again.'

'Yes, please,' said Jeremy James. 'When?'

'Whenevair you like,' said the man.

'Can we come tomorrow?' asked Jeremy James.

'You must ask your fazair,' said the man.

Jeremy James didn't know what a fazair was, but Daddy seemed to understand.

'We'll see you next time we're in London,' he said to the man.

'We're going to be in London tomorrow,' said Jeremy James.

Daddy had obviously forgotten that.

CHAPTER TEN

Wolf Watching

There were hundreds of people at the theatre, and unlike the Pry Monster, the taxi driver and the bushy man, they all seemed very happy. Maybe they'd been eating in bell towers as well.

Daddy and Jeremy James went up a broad staircase, Daddy showed his tickets to a smiling man at the door, and then they went inside a huge room that was full of purple seats. There was a purple curtain at one end of the theatre, and glass lamps hanging from the ceiling, and galleries and balconies and gold ornaments on all sides. Most of the seats were already sat in, and people were laughing and chattering, and Jeremy James noticed one lady with a box of chocolates in her hand. But even if she'd offered him one, he couldn't have eaten it. Not yet, anyway.

Jeremy James had been to theatres before. Once Daddy had had to talk to somebody, and Jeremy James had wandered on to the stage and had a chat with some of the actors. They hadn't been too pleased to see him, and one of them had carried him off the stage. The audience had liked seeing him, though, because they'd laughed and applauded. They'd also applauded on another occasion, when he and Daddy had gone on the stage with a magician named Marvello, who had smashed Daddy's watch, but hadn't really. Theatres were exciting places, and Jeremy James wondered if he'd be able to go up on this stage as well.

Daddy said excuse me to some people, who stood up and let them through to their seats. Jeremy James found himself sitting next to a lady with grey hair and a lot of sparkles round her neck.

'Hello,' said the lady.

'Hello,' said Jeremy James.

'What's your name?' she asked.

'Jeremy James,' said Jeremy James.

'And is this the first time you've been to the theatre, Jeremy James?' asked the lady.

'No,' said Jeremy James. 'I've been lots of times.'

At this moment, a tall man with a lot of hair sat right in front of Jeremy James.

'Can you see all right?' asked Daddy.

'Yes,' said Jeremy James. 'I can see a lot of hair.'

'Oh dear,' said Daddy. 'Here, try my seat.'

Daddy and Jeremy James changed places, but next to the tall man was a tall lady, and she had even more hair than the tall man.

'Can you see now?' asked Daddy.

'Yes,' said Jeremy James. 'I can see a lot more hair.'

The tall lady must have heard what Jeremy James had said, because she turned round in her seat.

'We're blocking your view, are we?' she said.

'The problem is,' said the sparkling lady with grey hair, 'that wherever Jeremy James sits, there'll be someone in front of him.'

'There's no one in front of us,' said the tall man, turning round. 'Let's all change places.'

'That's very kind of you,' said Daddy.

The tall man and the tall lady stood up, and then everybody in their row stood up to let them pass. And Daddy and Jeremy James also stood up, and everybody in their row stood up to let them pass as well. And just as the two rows were standing up, all the lights went out.

Jeremy James could see nothing in the sudden darkness, but he heard someone say 'Ouch!', and Daddy say 'Sorry!'

Jeremy James had just reached the end of the row when the lights went on again, the purple curtain swept open, and standing on the stage was a man dressed exactly like the little bald waiter in the bell tower.

'Are you all sitting comfortably?' he asked.

'No!' said Jeremy James.

A few people laughed.

'Sh!' said Daddy, excusing himself past the people in the next row.

'Good!' said the man. 'Then we can begin.'

'Not yet!' said Jeremy James.

A lot of people laughed.

'Jeremy James!' hissed Daddy. 'Sh!'

'But—'

'Sh!'

'Once upon a time,' said the man, 'in a deep dark forest, there lived a big bad wolf . . .'

Jeremy James sat down on his seat just as the big bad wolf came on to the stage, but Jeremy James could see straight away that it wasn't a wolf at all – it was a man dressed up as a wolf.

'I'm not a big bad wolf,' said the wolf.

'No, he's not,' said Jeremy James to Daddy. 'He's a man.'

'Sh!' said Daddy.

'I haven't had a decent meal in weeks,' said the wolf man, 'so I'm certainly not big. And what's bad about me? I'm one of the nicest wolves I know. So I'm not a big bad wolf at all. I'm a skinny nice wolf.'

From somewhere that Jeremy James couldn't see, an orchestra began to play, and the big bad skinny nice wolf man began to sing:

'Wolfie is my name,
Survival is my game,
I haven't had a bite in weeks,
Oh isn't it a shame!

Skinny as a feather,
I'm a piece of walking leather,
If I don't get my dinner soon,
I'll vanish altogether.'

On normal days, Jeremy James would have had a lot of sympathy for Wolfie, but tonight he didn't feel at all hungry.

'Red Riding Hood
Will be coming through the wood
With a basket full of goodies which I'd
Borrow if I could.'

It was when Wolfie mentioned the basket of goodies that Jeremy James suddenly felt a sharp pain in his tummy.

'Tender chicken breast,
Salad nicely dressed,
Cherry pie and ice cream,
A bottle of the best.'

'Daddy,' said Jeremy James.

'What is it?' whispered Daddy.

'I'm going to be sick,' said Jeremy James.

'What, now?' asked Daddy.

'Yes,' said Jeremy James.

'Hold on!' said Daddy.

He stood up, lifted Jeremy James from under the arms, and the whole row of people rose like a line of dominoes in reverse.

'Excuse me, sorry, excuse me, sorry...' said Daddy.

'Pickles in a jar,
Pot of caviar,
Half a pound of fudge cake,
And a chocolate bar.'

Daddy was racing up the aisle with Jeremy James over his shoulder and the nasty pain was getting nastier, and any second now . . .

Bang! Daddy had pushed open the door to the lavatory. Jeremy James leaned over, and out came a mixture of ice cream, jelly, tart, trifle, mousse, pie, pudding, chips and Willy's gallop.

'I shouldn't have let you eat so much,' said Daddy. 'No tummy in the world could have held on to all that dessert.'

Jeremy James had been sick once before. He'd eaten a whole box of liquorice allsorts, and Dr Bassett had come to the house to examine him. But Dr Bassett had said that Jeremy James had something called 'a touch of flu'.

'It wasn't the dessert, Daddy,' said Jeremy James. 'I've got a touch of flu.'

Daddy felt Jeremy James's forehead.

'Do you feel hot?' he asked.

'No,' said Jeremy James.

'Do you feel cold?' asked Daddy.

'No,' said Jeremy James.

'Do you feel like eating a bowlful of chocolate mousse, pie and ice cream?' asked Daddy.

Jeremy James thought for a moment.

'Not just yet,' he said.

'It's not a touch of flu,' said Daddy. 'It's a touch of over-eating.'

Then Daddy asked Jeremy James if he was feeling better, and Jeremy James said yes, and could they go back and watch the skinny nice wolf man again? But Daddy decided that they should go back to the hotel now because it was rather late, and actually he had a little bit of a pain in the tummy himself.

'Is over-eating catching, Daddy?' asked Jeremy James.

'It certainly is,' said Daddy.

As they left the theatre, the skinny nice wolf man

had just made his way to Granny's house, and the man in the black jacket and bow tie was telling the audience that Granny was sick. Maybe she had a touch of over-eating, too.

CHAPTER ELEVEN

Ampuluses

When Daddy and Jeremy James got back to the hotel, the bushy man was still sitting at his table, and his bottle was almost empty.

'Did you . . . hic . . . have a good time?' he asked.

'Yes, thank you,' said Jeremy James. 'I've been sick.'

'Sho have I,' said the man.

'I had a touch of over-eating,' said Jeremy James.

'That'sh funny,' said the man. 'I had a touch of over-drinkin'. Shame thing, more or lesh. What a life!'

Daddy and Jeremy James left him sitting there. Daddy was in quite a hurry to go upstairs, because the pain in his tummy had got worse, and so as soon as they'd gone into Room 33, he went out again.

Jeremy James sat on the bed and looked round the room. There wasn't very much to look at. There wasn't very much to do, either. He bounced on the bed a couple of times, and then went across to Daddy's bed and bounced on that, but the beds weren't very bouncy, and in any case bouncing on beds wasn't all that interesting.

The wardrobe wasn't interesting either. There was nothing in it except dust. The ceiling was boring, the walls were boring, the brown curtains were boring, the wash basin was very boring, the chair was boring, the table was boring . . . except that on the table was the telephone. The telephone wasn't boring. No, the telephone was really interesting.

Jeremy James wandered across to the table and looked at the telephone. Ever since he'd spoken to the lady hundreds of miles away, he'd been forbidden to do any dialling. But that was at home. This telephone wasn't at home. This telephone was in the hotel. Daddy wouldn't have to pay the bill for the telephone in the hotel, would he?

Jeremy James climbed up on to the chair, so that he could have a closer look at the telephone. It was a nice telephone. Brown, like the curtains. And with numbers. There, for instance, was the 0 that Daddy had got him to press before he'd spoken to the bushy man.

Jeremy James wondered if someone might already be talking on the telephone. There was certainly no harm in just picking it up and listening. And so he picked up the receiver. There was a humming noise.

If he were to press the 0, the bushy man would say: 'What a life!' It wouldn't be much fun talking to the bushy man. If you wanted to talk to somebody else, you had to press 9. That was how you got really interesting conversations.

Jeremy James pressed the 9. The humming sound stopped, but nothing else happened, and so he pressed 9 again. There was a click, but that was all. He pressed again. Another click. Once more, thought Jeremy James, and pressed the 9 again.

There was a very short *brrr*, and then a woman's voice said: 'What service do you want? Police, fire or ambulance?'

This was a bit of a surprise for Jeremy James, because he hadn't realized that he wanted any service, and now he had a choice of three.

'What service do you want, caller?' asked the woman again. 'Police, fire or ambulance?'

'Police,' he said. They'd be the most fun to talk to.

'What is your name, caller?' asked the woman.

That was an easy question.

'Jeremy James,' said Jeremy James.

'Telephone number?'

That wasn't such an easy question. Jeremy James didn't know.

'Can you give me your telephone number?' asked the woman.

That was an easy question again.

'No,' said Jeremy James.

'Where are you, Jeremy James?'

Another easy question.

'Hotel Jeremy,' he said.

There were some clicks, and then a man's voice came on the line.

'Police,' said the man.

'Hello, police,' said Jeremy James.

'What's the trouble, son?' asked the man.

This was one of the difficult questions. Jeremy James didn't know of any trouble. And so he didn't answer.

'I understand you're in a hotel, is that right?' said the man.

'Yes,' said Jeremy James.

'Who's with you?'

'Nobody.'

'You're all alone?'

'Yes.'

There was a slight pause, and then the man asked where Mummy was. Jeremy James told him that she was at home. Next he asked where Daddy was, and Jeremy James started to say that he'd gone . . . well, he was going to tell the man that Daddy had gone to the lavatory, but grown-ups don't like talking about lavatories, and so Jeremy James simply said, 'He's gone', and left it at that.

'Gone?' echoed the policeman.

'He had a pain,' explained Jeremy James.

'He had a pain and he's gone?' cried the policeman.

Then Jeremy James heard him say to someone: 'Ring for an ambulance, quick!' Next the policeman asked Jeremy James if he knew the number of the room he was in, and Jeremy James told him it was 33.

'Stay right there, Jeremy James,' said the policeman. 'We'll be with you in a minute.'

The telephone went very quiet, and so Jeremy James put it down. It was very kind of the policeman to say he'd come, and that would certainly be a nice surprise for Daddy. But it seemed a bit silly to ring for an ambulance as well, because they'd never be able to get an ambulance up the stairs to Room 33. Unless perhaps the policeman was going to take Jeremy James downstairs to look at the ambulance. Jeremy James wondered what exactly ambulances were for. He'd seen them in the street – they were big and white, and sometimes flashed their lights and made loud pah-pah noises, but what did people do in them?

Daddy came into the room. He was a little pale.

'Daddy, what are ampuluses for?' asked Jeremy James.

Daddy stretched out on his bed.

'What are what for?' he asked.

'Ampuluses.'

'What are ampuluses?' asked Daddy.

'Big white cars that flash their lights and go pah-pah,' said Jeremy James.

'Oh, ambulances,' said Daddy. 'They take sick people to hospital. What made you ask . . .?'

At that very moment, there were loud pah-pah

noises from the street, and they seemed to come right outside the hotel before they stopped.

'Well, I'm blowed!' said Daddy. 'What a coincidence! That sounds like an ambulance arriving at the hotel. Unless it's the police. Fancy that! Just when you were asking about them!'

Daddy was even more surprised when half a minute later there was a knock on the door, and in came one policeman, one policewoman, and two men carrying a stretcher.

'Oh!' said Daddy.

'Ah!' said the policeman.

'Hello,' said Jeremy James.

'You must be Jeremy James,' said the policeman.

'Yes,' said Jeremy James.

'And are you his father, sir?' the policeman asked Daddy.

'Yes, of course I am,' said Daddy.

'And you're not dead, sir?'

'No, not as far as I know.'

'Dying, perhaps, sir?'

'No.'

'Slightly ill, maybe?'

'Well,' said Daddy, 'I did have a bit of an upset stomach. Do you mind telling me what this is all about?'

'Excuse me,' said one of the men with the stretcher, 'but do you need an ambulance or don't you?'

'It doesn't look as if we do,' said the policeman.

'Then we'll be on our way,' said the stretcher man.

The two men with the stretcher left, and the police-man took out a notebook and wrote something down in it.

'I wish you'd tell me what's going on,' said Daddy.

'I think, sir,' said the policeman, 'that maybe your son should tell us *all* what's going on.'

Jeremy James began to have a strange feeling that whatever was going on should not have been going on. The policeman certainly hadn't come to play games or to show him what ampuluses were for, and if he were to ask now what the trouble was, Jeremy James would be able to tell him. The trouble was what Jeremy James was in. Daddy was looking at him, the policeman was looking at him, and the policewoman was looking at him, and the look with which they were looking at him had an almost ma-gical effect on his eyes. One moment they were com-pletely dry, and the next they were full of tears, which at once started to trickle down his face. And the magic spread to his bottom lip, which began to go all wiggly . . .

'It's all right,' said the policewoman, kneeling down beside him. 'There's no need to cry.'

Jeremy James thought there was every need to cry. It was not only that he actually felt like crying, but also it seemed to him that the more he cried, the less he'd have to explain.

'I know what happened,' said the policewoman. 'Your Daddy had a pain, didn't he?'

Jeremy James nodded tearfully.

'And then he went out and left you alone. Is that right?'

Jeremy James nodded tearfully.

'And when he didn't come back, you thought something terrible had happened, didn't you?'

Jeremy James hadn't thought any such thing, but he was getting into the swing of things now, so he nodded tearfully.

'And then you rang nine-nine-nine to get some help for him.'

Jeremy James nodded tearfully.

The policewoman stood up and rested her hand on Jeremy James's shoulder.

'I think,' she said, 'that Jeremy James is a very clever boy. He thought his Daddy was dying, and he wanted to save him. Isn't that right, Jeremy James?'

Jeremy James nodded not quite so tearfully. He liked having the policewoman's hand on his shoulder. Somehow it made him feel that even if he was in trouble, trouble couldn't get to him.

'That sounds very possible,' said the policeman, who then looked rather severely at Daddy. 'But if that's true, sir, you shouldn't have left the little boy on his own.'

'Well, officer,' said Daddy, 'where I was going, I could hardly have taken him with me.'

'Anyway, I'm glad you're not as "gone" as we thought you were, sir. And as for you, young man,' said the policeman looking down at Jeremy James, who looked up at the policeman, 'we could do with bright lads like you in the police force, so if you ever need a job, come and see us.'

Jeremy James's eyes dried as magically as they had moistened.

'Yes, please!' he said. 'I *would* like a job!'

'Well, not just yet,' said the policeman. 'You'd better grow up first, or the helmet won't fit you.'

Then the policeman and policewoman said good-bye to Daddy and Jeremy James, and the police-woman gave Jeremy James a kiss, so he gave her a big kiss in return. She'd earned it.

'You didn't really think anything had happened to me, did you?' said Daddy when they'd gone.

Jeremy James looked at the floor.

'You were playing with the telephone, weren't you?'

Jeremy James wished he had the policewoman's hand on his shoulder again.

'And what have you been told about telephones?'

'I mustn't play with them,' said Jeremy James, still studying the carpet.

'Lucky for you that you had such a good lawyer,' said Daddy, 'or we'd really have been in trouble. Now, do you promise never to play with telephones again?'

'I promise,' said Jeremy James.

'Right,' said Daddy. 'Then let's have a wash and go to bed.'

Jeremy James would have liked to say, 'Oh no, not another wash!' But instead, he said, 'Yes, Daddy.'

When he'd had his wash and brushed his teeth, Daddy tucked him up in bed and turned the light out.

All the same, thought Jeremy James, as he lay there in the darkness, something *might* have happened to Daddy, and if something *had* happened to Daddy, he'd have been pleased that Jeremy James had dialled 999. And the policewoman would have been right to say how clever Jeremy James was.

'The policewoman was the nicest person in London, wasn't she, Daddy?' said Jeremy James.

But Daddy was fast asleep. He'd had a very tiring day.

CHAPTER TWELVE

Breakfast

Jeremy James was looking forward to breakfast. He and Daddy went downstairs to the breakfast room, where there were about a dozen tables, most of which had one or two grey-suited men sitting at them. Daddy and Jeremy James sat in a corner and waited.

After a few minutes, a thin, long-faced woman with wispy brown hair and a white apron came in carrying a tray, which she put in front of a fat, bald-headed man at the next table. Then she turned to Daddy and Jeremy James.

'What do you want for breakfast?' she asked.

'Egg and bacon,' said Jeremy James. 'Please.'

'You'll be lucky,' said the woman. 'Coffee or tea?'

Daddy said he'd have coffee, and Jeremy James would have orange juice, and the woman nodded and went away.

'Some funny goings-on here last night,' said the fat man at the next table.

'Oh?' said Daddy. 'What sort of goings-on?'

'The police were here, and an ambulance.'

'Really?' said Daddy.

'Yes,' said the man. 'Strange business. The owner got drunk and fell down the cellar steps. Only the police and ambulance hadn't come for him at all.'

'Hadn't they?' said Daddy.

'No,' said the fat man. 'Somebody else had sent for them, but that was a false alarm. Then just as the ambulance men were going out, they saw the cellar door open and heard somebody groaning. Poor chap had broken an arm *and* a leg. I came in when they were taking him out. Amazing stroke of luck that someone had just dialled nine-nine-nine.'

'It certainly was,' said Daddy.

'I dialled nine-nine-nine,' said Jeremy James.

'Did you?' asked the man.

'He did it by accident,' said Daddy.

'That's how the owner fell down the steps,' said the man. 'By accident. Broken arm and leg. What a life, eh?'

'I expect that's what he said, too,' remarked Daddy.

'The waitress is his wife,' whispered the fat man.

Daddy said he thought the owner's wife had left him, but the fat man said she'd come back when she heard about the accident.

'She hates this place,' he said. 'Can't blame her, either. Who'd want a job in a place like this with a man like that? Now he's going to be off for weeks, and she's stuck here till she can get someone to take over. That's why she's in such a vile mood.'

The long-faced woman came in with a tray, which she put down on the table in front of Daddy and Jeremy James. On it were a cup of coffee, a glass of orange juice, and four bread rolls with some butter and marmalade.

'Where's breakfast?' asked Jeremy James.

'That's it,' said the woman, and went away.

'It's what they call a Continental breakfast,' said Daddy.

'I don't want a conky mental breakfast,' said Jeremy James. 'I want a real breakfast.'

The fat man hadn't wanted a conky mental breakfast either, but apparently everybody had to have the same because it was the owner who always did the cooking, and now he was in hospital.

'You seem to know a lot about this hotel,' said Daddy.

'Oh I do,' said the fat man. 'And I'll tell you something else. My room hadn't been cleaned.'

'Ah, well,' said Daddy. 'I can tell *you* something about that. The chambermaid left last week.'

'I know,' said the fat man. 'No chambermaid ever stays in this place more than a few weeks. And frankly, one night's enough for me. But I shall feel really sorry for the owner when he comes out of hospital.'

'Why?' asked Daddy.

'Because he's going to find himself in even worse trouble,' said the fat man.

Daddy said that, considering the owner was in hospital with a broken arm and leg, his wife was going to leave him, the chambermaid *had* left him, he couldn't pay his mortgage, and the lift wasn't working, he might have difficulty finding any more trouble to get into.

'You'd be surprised,' said the fat man. 'Just when you've slid to the bottom of the hill, that's when the avalanche hits you.'

'What's his next bit of trouble, then?' asked Daddy.

'Me,' said the fat man. 'I'm a hotel inspector.'

CHAPTER THIRTEEN

Dinosaurs

Daddy and Jeremy James were to meet Mrs Robinson, the important lady, for lunch, and so Daddy said they would leave their bags in the car and spend the morning at the Natural History Museum.

After the breakfast-that-wasn't-a-breakfast, they packed their bags and went downstairs to pay the bill. The long-faced lady – now without her apron – was sitting at the table.

'We'd like to pay,' said Daddy.

'Not many people would,' said the lady.

She looked in a book, wrote something down on a piece of paper, gave it to Daddy, and Daddy gave her some money.

'How's your husband?' he asked.

'Plastered,' she said, 'one way or another. Was it your little boy that rang for the ambulance?'

'That's right,' said Daddy.

Jeremy James waited for her to say thank you, and what a clever boy, and here's your reward.

'With all that whisky in him,' she said, 'you should have sent for the fire brigade.'

Daddy and Jeremy James said goodbye to her, and set off for the car park.

'I think I know why London people are so unhappy,' said Jeremy James.

'Why?' asked Daddy.

'Because,' said Jeremy James, 'they don't eat a real breakfast.'

When they'd left their cases in the car, they went on the underground again, and from the underground station walked to the Natural History Museum. This turned out to be another palace, and as they walked through the door, Jeremy James found himself looking out for the Queen. But what he actually saw was a hundred times more eye-wide-opening than even the Queen. Standing ahead of him, in a vast hall, was the biggest animal he had ever seen.

To be more precise, it was the skeleton of the biggest animal he had ever seen. If it hadn't been an animal, it might have been a ship, it was so huge.

'What is it, Daddy?' gasped Jeremy James.

'It's a dinosaur,' said Daddy. 'It's called Diplodocus.'

'Dipperdopus!' said Jeremy James.

'It's one of the biggest animals that ever lived,' said Daddy.

They stepped into the hall, and gazed up at the mighty monster. The cage of its ribs could have held twenty lions, and you could have stood a church on the pillars of its legs. The tail was almost as long as the body, and stretched all the way down to the floor. As for the bones of the neck, they reached out like another tail that extended along the ceiling until it ended up in a surprisingly tiny head.

'Why has it got such a small head, Daddy?' asked Jeremy James.

'Because if its head was any bigger,' said Daddy, 'its neck would fall down.'

'I wish I was a Dipperdopus!' said Jeremy James.

'If you were,' said Daddy, 'I don't know what we'd give you for breakfast.'

'A thousand eggs and bacon,' said Jeremy James.

He asked Daddy if there were any Dipperdopuses wandering around London, but Daddy said the Dipperdopus had been dead for 150 million years.

'What did it die of?' asked Jeremy James.

'Overweight, I expect,' said Daddy.

When Jeremy James finally took his wide eyes off the Dipperdopus, they came to rest on a quite amazing head that was nearby. It was the sort of head any monster would be proud of. It was thick and heavy, with staring, glaring eyes and massive jaws that were open in a grin you might expect from the Devil. But what was truly terrifying was its teeth. They were as long and sharp and pointed as a row of daggers, and Jeremy James guessed that with a single crunch of those teeth, the monster could have cracked a thousand lollipops. With a head like that, it wouldn't need to kill its enemies – they'd die of fright just looking at it.

'Tyrannosaurus,' said Daddy. 'The fiercest of all the dinosaurs.'

'He ought to be in the Chamber of Horace,' said Jeremy James.

It was a pity Tyrannosaurus had lost his body, and Jeremy James wondered what had happened to it.

'He probably ate it,' said Daddy.

'If the Runny Roarus had a fight with the Dopey Dippus,' said Jeremy James, 'who would win?'

'Well, the Diplodocus might just possibly squash the Tyrannosaurus,' said Daddy, 'but my guess is that the Tyrannosaurus would eat the Diplodocus. And afterwards die of indigestion.'

Diplodocus and Tyrannosaurus weren't the only dinosaurs in the hall, and the dinosaurs weren't the only monsters in the museum. In another hall was the biggest animal in the world – a blue whale – and Daddy said there were still blue whales swimming in the sea today. But although the blue whale was as hugely huge as London, it didn't have the mighty legs of a Diplodocus, or the fearsome teeth of a Tyrannosaurus. And although Daddy took Jeremy James to other rooms that were full of birds, and creepy-crawlies, and human beings, none of them had Diplodocus legs or Tyrannosaurus teeth either. What Jeremy James really wanted to do was to go and have another look at the dinosaurs.

When they got back into the dinosaur hall, the first thing Jeremy James noticed was a smartly dressed lady with a feathery hat, and a ginger-headed boy with freckles. The lady was looking up at Diplodocus, and the ginger-headed boy was baring his teeth and snarling at Tyrannosaurus.

'Look, Daddy!' said Jeremy James. 'It's Timothy and Mrs Smy-Fossycoo!'

The Smyth-Fortescues lived next door. Timothy was a year older than Jeremy James, and he was believed to be the cleverest boy in the world – though he was the only person who believed it.

'Hello, Mrs Smyth-Fortescue. Hello, Timothy,' said Daddy. 'Fancy meeting you here.'

'Oh, what a coincidence!' said Mrs Smyth-Fortescue. 'We've just dropped Mr Smyth-Fortescue at the airport – one of his business trips, you know

– and I thought I'd bring dear Timothy here. He does so love the animals . . .'

While Mrs Smyth-Fortescue talked and Daddy listened, Jeremy James and Timothy wandered around the Diplodocus.

'I bet you don't know what it's called,' said Timothy.

'Yes I do,' replied Jeremy James. 'It's a Dippy Dopus.'

'No it's not,' said Timothy. 'It's a skelington.'

'It's not. It's a Dippy Dopus.'

'You don't know anything.'

'Yes I do. I know how long Dippy Dopus has been dead.'

'It's not a Dippy Dopus,' said Timothy. '*You're* a Dippy Dopus. That's a skelington, and how long has it been dead?'

'A million hundred and fifty years.'

'No, it hasn't.'

'Yes it has, because Daddy said so. Go and ask him.'

Timothy looked across to where Daddy and Mrs Smyth-Fortescue were chatting.

'Who cares?' he said. 'Nobody cares how long a skelington's been dead.'

Jeremy James cared. Because he knew that it *was* a Dippy Dopus, and it *did* die a million hundred and fifty years ago. And Timothy always pretended he knew everything, but he didn't.

'Well I know something else too,' said Jeremy James.

'What?' asked Timothy.

'Not telling,' said Jeremy James.

' 'Cos you don't know anything.'

'Yes I do.'

'Tell us then if you know, but you don't.'

'I know,' said Jeremy James, 'that Dippy Dopus is one of the biggest animals that ever lived.'

'No it's not.'

'Yes it is.'

'I've seen animals a lot bigger than that.'

'No you haven't.'

'Yes I have.'

'Where?'

Again Timothy looked across at Daddy and Mrs Smyth-Fortescue, and then he lowered his voice.

'In America,' he said. 'They've got animals ten times bigger than that in America.'

'They can't have,' said Jeremy James.

'Yes they have. In America everything's bigger than it is here. This skelington's small compared to the animals they've got in America. In America kids like you go for rides on little animals like this.'

'You couldn't ride a Dippy Dopus!' gasped Jeremy James.

'People ride them all the time in America,' said Timothy.

'*Nobody* could ride a Dippy Dopus!'

'It's easy.'

Jeremy James said it was impossible. Timothy said he'd ridden animals ten times bigger than the skelington, Jeremy James said Timothy couldn't even ride *this* skelington, and Timothy said yes he could, and just watch me.

Then he did something Jeremy James thought he ought not to have done. Around the Diplodocus was a sort of low glass wall, and Timothy suddenly clambered over the low glass wall and ran to the dinosaur's tail.

'Hey! Come back!' shouted an angry voice, but before the owner of the voice – a man with fiery eyes and a furry moustache – could stop him, Timothy was already climbing up the tail.

The fiery, furry man leapt over the low glass wall, and shouted: 'Get off of there right now!' But Timothy was out of his reach, and simply went on climbing.

'Oh dear!' said Mrs Smyth-Fortescue. 'It's my Timothy!'

'Oh dear!' said Daddy. 'So it is!'

Now everyone was looking at the ginger-headed boy making his way on all fours up the Diplodocus's tail. And as Timothy reached the top of the tail, he suddenly looked down and saw everybody looking up.

'What's he doing up there?' asked Daddy, who had come round to stand with Jeremy James.

'He said he could ride Dippy Dopus,' replied Jeremy James, 'and I said he couldn't.'

'It looks as if you were right,' said Daddy.

Timothy was now holding on to the bones round about where the dinosaur's bottom would have been if he'd had one, and Timothy's freckled face had turned rather white.

'Who does that child belong to?' shouted the fiery, furry man.

'Erm well, oh dear, he's mine!' said Mrs Smyth-Fortescue.

'Then tell him to come down!'

'Timothy, darling!' called Mrs Smyth-Fortescue. 'Come down now, please, there's a good boy!'

'I can't!' cried Timothy.

'Yes, you can, darling!' called Mrs Smyth-Fortescue.

'I'm stuck!' cried Timothy, and even from down below, Jeremy James could see the freckled face beginning to crumple.

'You'll be in trouble for this!' roared the fiery, furry man in the sort of voice you might expect from a Tyrannosaurus.

'Help!' howled Timothy – though it wasn't clear whether he needed help because he couldn't get down, or help because he was going to be in trouble.

At this moment anyway, help arrived, in the shape of two uniformed men carrying a ladder.

'Stay where you are, son!' called one of the men.

Timothy was in no state to do anything else.

The men placed the ladder against the leg of the Diplodocus, and then while one of them kept the

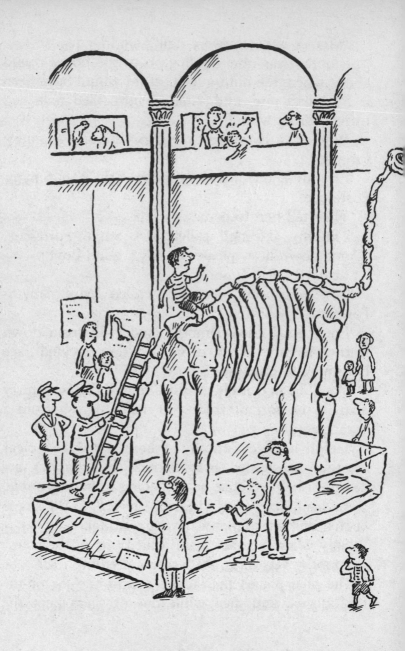

ladder steady, the other climbed up. There was a great cheer as he caught hold of Timothy, draped him over his shoulder, and climbed down again.

Timothy had closed his eyes very tight as the man had carried him down, but when they reached the floor, he opened them again and looked straight at Jeremy James.

'I told you you couldn't ride him,' said Jeremy James.

Mrs Smyth-Fortescue took Timothy from the arms of the man who had rescued him.

'There, there, darling!' she said. 'Are you all right?'

'The question, madam,' said the Tyrannosaurus man, 'is whether the dinosaur is all right. If not, it's going to cost you a packet. Now if you and your little darling would just follow me . . .'

'Oh dear,' said Mrs Smyth-Fortescue. 'I'm sure Timothy didn't mean any harm.'

She nodded goodbye to Daddy and Jeremy James, and Timothy lifted his head long enough to poke out his tongue at Jeremy James. Then they made their way through quite a large crowd of people – some of whom were laughing while others were shaking their heads – and disappeared through a door that was marked 'Private'.

'I know why Timothy couldn't ride it,' said Jeremy James.

'Why?' asked Daddy.

'Because,' said Jeremy James, 'he didn't know it was a Dippy Dopus. He thought it was a skelington.'

Daddy laughed and said that dinosaurs were not for riding anyway, and buses and trains were, and it was time they went for lunch with Mrs Robinson.

CHAPTER FOURTEEN

Mrs Robinson

Jeremy James had never seen so many books. Daddy's books at home were all over the place, but in Mrs Robinson's office there were books all over the books that were all over the place. There were shelves and piles and boxes and tablefuls of them. And in the middle of this one-room library was a desk, in front of which sat Daddy, with Jeremy James standing beside him, and behind which sat little Mrs Robinson. She had grey hair tied in a bun, a tiny turned-up nose, and very soft cheeks down which two thin lines of tears were trickling.

'I'm sorry, John,' she was saying, 'but I've got some awful news. I've been given the sack.'

Daddy said, 'Oh!' and looked very serious.

'I just don't know what I'm going to do,' said Mrs Robinson.

Jeremy James looked round the room, but he could see no sign of a sack. All he could see were books. Maybe the sack had got hidden under the books. What he couldn't understand, though, was why getting a sack should be so awful. Father Christmas

brought a sack round at Christmas time, and everybody was very pleased to see him. Jeremy James would have liked a whole sack to himself.

'Daddy,' whispered Jeremy James, while Mrs Robinson wiped her eyes with her handkerchief. 'If Mrs Robinson doesn't want it, can I have it?'

'Have what, Jeremy James?' asked Daddy.

'The sack,' said Jeremy James.

'Getting the sack,' said Daddy, 'means losing your job.'

Mrs Robinson had heard the questions, and laughed in spite of her tears.

'Sorry, Fiona,' said Daddy, 'but I suppose it is a funny expression.'

'Did you think it was a sack of toys, Jeremy James?' asked Mrs Robinson.

'Yes,' said Jeremy James.

'I wish it was,' said Mrs Robinson. 'Then I'd give it to you with pleasure.'

She explained to Daddy that the company had been taken over by another company, and the new owners already had someone – a much younger person – to do her job, so they didn't need her any more. She'd been given a month's notice, and would be able to finish her work on Daddy's book, but then she'd have to find another job.

'And that won't be easy at my age,' she said.

Daddy said several times how sorry he was, and how he wished he could help her, and Jeremy James wished he could help her, too.

'Anyway,' said Mrs Robinson, 'it's lunchtime. Are you hungry, Jeremy James?'

Jeremy James was as hungry as a dinosaur, and as they left Mrs Robinson's office, he whispered to Daddy: 'Can we go to the bell tower?'

Daddy shook his head.

'Why not?' whispered Jeremy James.

'Because we're going somewhere else,' whispered Daddy.

The three of them walked down Welbeck Street, turned left, turned right, turned left again, and . . .

'Oh look!' cried Jeremy James. 'It's our hotel!'

Jeremy James was quite pleased to see the hotel again – until he remembered something . . .

'But they've only got rolls and marmalade!' he said.

'Don't worry, we're not going there for lunch,' said Mrs Robinson.

The place where they did go for lunch was full of gold dragons and lanterns and beautiful wiggly lamps. What it didn't seem to have was a cabinet full of mousses, puddings, pies, etc., and it turned out that they didn't have chicken and chips or Willy's gallop either. What they did have, though, was a delicious bowl of rice with all kinds of things in it. There were pieces of chicken, egg, various vegetables, shrimps, and green bits, red bits, and yellow bits. Each mouthful tasted different, and although it was a pity there weren't any chips, it was certainly the best meal Jeremy James had eaten since last night's dinner at Le Campanile.

Every so often during the meal, Jeremy James noticed Mrs Robinson wiping a tear from her eye, and his mind would wander from his bowl to her sack. If only he could find her a job, then she wouldn't have to be yet another of those unhappy London people – but how did people get jobs? The policeman had said that the police force needed bright lads, but Mrs Robinson wasn't a lad. Besides, he'd said that Jeremy James would have to grow up first or the helmet wouldn't fit him, and little Mrs Robinson certainly hadn't grown enough for the helmet to fit her.

The rice was followed by ice cream – several different flavours which helped to take Jeremy James's mind off the job again. But when the last mouthful had melted away, and the spoon had been licked clean, twice on both sides, Jeremy James suddenly had an idea. It came into his head almost as if someone had fed it to him. He could hardly wait for Daddy and Mrs Robinson to finish their conversation and their coffee.

At last the three of them stepped out into the street, and Jeremy James wished they could walk on the right side. If they didn't, it was going to be very difficult for him to get Mrs Robinson a job. He was lucky – or rather, Mrs Robinson was lucky. They *were* on the right side. He held on to Daddy's hand, and while Daddy talked to Mrs Robinson, Jeremy James waited and waited until the moment came.

'Hey! Jeremy James!' cried Daddy, as Jeremy James suddenly let go of his hand and raced away.

As they were on the right side, he didn't have to race far. With half a dozen steps, he was through the open door of Hotel Jeremy, and running along the hallway. As he ran, he wished very, very hard that the long-faced, wispy-haired woman would be sitting at the table where the bushy man had sat. It must have been wishes-come-true day, because there she was, as miserable as she'd been at breakfast.

'Forgotten something, have you?' she asked, as Jeremy James skidded to a halt in front of her.

'No,' said Jeremy James. 'Is the bushy man still in hospital?'

'My husband, you mean,' said the woman. 'Yes, of course he is.'

'And you don't want to do his job, do you?' said Jeremy James.

'No,' answered the woman.

'So can you give his job to Mrs Robinson?' asked Jeremy James.

At this moment, Daddy arrived.

'Please!' pleaded Jeremy James.

The long-faced woman looked from Jeremy James to Daddy and back to Jeremy James.

'Who's Mrs Robinson?' she asked.

'She's the lady with the sack,' said Jeremy James.

'What's going on?' asked Daddy.

'Well,' said the woman, 'your little boy's just asked me to give my job to Mrs Robinson, who's the lady with the sack.'

Daddy looked long and hard at Jeremy James, and suddenly burst out laughing. He quickly explained to the long-faced woman all about Mrs Robinson's sack, and then something quite extraordinary happened. The woman's long face became shorter and wider, and the droopy corners of her mouth began to go up instead of down, and her eyes – which had been as dull as rolls and marmalade – became as shiny as fried eggs. Then her lips opened, and out came a laugh even louder than Daddy's. Jeremy James had never seen a face change so quickly. It was like the sun coming out from behind a cloud.

'Come on, Jeremy James,' said Daddy. 'Poor Mrs Robinson'll be wondering what's happened.'

'But she hasn't got the job yet!' said Jeremy James. 'Please can she have the job? Please!'

The shorter-and-wider-faced woman reached across the table and ruffled Jeremy James's hair.

'Of course she can have it,' she said. 'But only if she wants it.'

'Thank you!' cried Jeremy James, and danced out of Hotel Jeremy, leaving the woman sitting back in her chair, shaking her head and smiling.

But Mrs Robinson didn't want the job. She had a little cry when Daddy told her what had happened, and Daddy had to explain to Jeremy James that Mrs Robinson wanted to do book work and not hotel work.

'She could put all her books in the hotel!' said Jeremy James. 'She'd have more room for them there!'

'That's true,' said Daddy, 'but she wouldn't have time to read them.'

Mrs Robinson had dried her eyes, and crouched down beside Jeremy James.

'Thank you very, very much, Jeremy James,' she said. 'I'll never forget what you've just done for me. And I feel a lot better knowing there's a job here if I want it.'

Jeremy James was pleased that she felt better, and it seemed to him that working in a hotel could be a lot of fun. You could talk to people on the telephone, for one thing. And for another, you could make sure that everybody had eggs and bacon for their breakfast. If he'd been Mrs Robinson, he'd have taken the job straight away. But even though Mrs Robinson was very small, she was grown-up, and grown-ups can be as strange as dinosaurs.

'We'd better tell the lady that Mrs Robinson doesn't want the job,' he said rather sadly.

'I think,' said Daddy, 'the lady already knows.'

When they got back to Welbeck Street, Mrs Robinson asked them to come to her office. There she went to a pile of books behind another pile of books beside a box of books under a table of books, and pulled out a book. It was a very big book.

'This, Jeremy James,' she said, 'is for you.'

She handed it over to him, and on the front cover was a picture that he recognized immediately.

'It's Dippy Dopus!' he cried. 'Look, Daddy, it's Dippy Dopus! Thank you very, very much, Mrs Robinson!'

He gave Mrs Robinson an even bigger kiss than he'd given to the policewoman, and when he'd kissed her, he noticed that she was smiling. Like the long-faced woman, she suddenly seemed brighter and sunnier.

Daddy and Jeremy James said goodbye to Mrs Robinson, and went out into the street. Jeremy James was holding his big book of dinosaurs under one arm, and his other hand was in Daddy's.

'London people are not happy,' said Jeremy James as they walked towards the car park, 'but they *could* be happy if they did a bit more smiling.'

CHAPTER FIFTEEN

Goodbye, London

Surprisingly, the car park had not moved from where it had been before, and the car had stayed in exactly the same space where they had left it. Daddy and Jeremy James found them both with no trouble at all.

'I'm learning,' said Daddy. 'The secret, Jeremy James, is to make mental notes of where things are. You don't just leave things and walk away. You say to yourself: "This is where it is", and then afterwards you remember. Simple. Now then, where's the parking ticket?'

Unfortunately, Daddy had forgotten to remember where the parking ticket was. He soon found where it was not. It was not in his coat or his jacket or his trousers. Nor was it in his bag. It wasn't in Jeremy James's bag either. And it wasn't on the front seat of the car, or the back seat, and it wasn't on the ledge under the windscreen, and it wasn't in the glove compartment.

'I must have lost it,' said Daddy.

Jeremy James thought Daddy must have lost it,

too, because otherwise, why were they looking for it? It was while Daddy was searching through his pockets for the fifth time that Jeremy James discovered where he had lost it. Jeremy James was sitting in the driver's seat, holding the steering wheel. As he couldn't see through the windscreen, he leaned over to look out of the open driver's door, and happened to notice that there was a pocket in the door. Sticking out of the pocket was a very tickety looking piece of paper.

'Is this it, Daddy?' asked Jeremy James.

'Of course!' said Daddy. 'I put it in there so that I wouldn't lose it!'

Daddy next applied his clever new method to finding the way out of London. He sat in the car and studied the map, memorizing directions and names of roads.

'I think I've got it,' he said at last. 'Concentration and memory, that's how to do it.'

He strapped Jeremy James into his seat, started the car, and away they went up the twisty tunnel as far as the exit barrier. There Daddy paid something called 'a small fortune', the barrier rose, and they drove the rest of the way up the street.

'Ah!' said Daddy. 'Now then, is it left, or is it right?'

Daddy's clever new method led to the same result as his old method, and soon they were driving through whatever streets of London happened to be in front of them. Jeremy James was no longer interested in the streets of London, though. He was busy watching his old friend Diplodocus munching a mouthful of grass from a riverbank, while on the other side of the page his old friend Tyrannosaurus was munching a mouthful of neck from a Deadosaurus.

At least, Jeremy James thought he was watching them. But twice he suddenly found his book of dinosaurs lying on the seat beside him. The first occasion was when he woke up just in time for some refreshments at the motorway service station. He was very good at waking up for refreshments. He was good at making them disappear, too. His old friends Diplodocus and Tyrannosaurus could not have munched the egg sandwich or the chocolate fudge cake any more efficiently than Jeremy James did.

On the second occasion, the car had stopped outside the house that he knew and loved better than any other house in the world. Mummy had already opened the front door, and gave him a hug and a kiss as he bounded in.

'Jem Jem home Londy!' cried Jennifer, leaping to her feet in the playpen and shaking the bars.

'Jem Jem Londy,' said Christopher, sitting beside her.

Going away was nice, but Jeremy James decided that coming home was even nicer. Then Mummy told him to go and have a wash, and he wondered if perhaps going away was nicer after all.

'Well, Jeremy James,' said Mummy, as they sat at

the table that evening, 'what did you like most in London?'

Jeremy James thought hard.

'The Dippy Dopus,' he said, 'and the bell tower, and Mrs Robinson.'

'And what did you like least?' asked Daddy.

'The Pry Monster,' said Jeremy James. 'And breakfast.'

He told Mummy all about the things he and Daddy had seen and done, and the people they'd met. She laughed about the pigeon lady and Number Coo, she gasped at the story of Polly Tishuns, she said 'Ts, ts!' about Timothy riding the dinosaur, she smiled at how Jeremy James had tried to get Mrs Robinson a job, and he didn't tell her about dialling nine-nine-nine.

'Of course,' said Daddy, 'there were loads of things we didn't see. We never went to the zoo, or the Tower of London, or St Paul's Cathedral, or Westminster Abbey.'

'You'd need to spend at least a week there to see *all* the sights,' said Mummy.

'Then we'd need to spend two weeks,' said Jeremy James.

'Why two weeks?' asked Mummy

'One week to see them,' said Jeremy James, 'and one week for Daddy to find them.'

David Henry Wilson
Do Goldfish Play the Violin?

'In that game of Freezing,' said Daddy, 'what exactly did you throw in the goldfish pond?'

'The black box,' said Jeremy James.

'What black box?' asked Daddy.

'The one with Melissa's violin,' said Jeremy James.

Jeremy James is very good at solving problems like Melissa's violin, lost car keys and a missing Virgin Mary. But when it comes to paying bills, falling in the river, and turning yellow and purple, Jeremy James himself can be a bit of a problem . . .

David Henry Wilson
Do Gerbils Go To Heaven?

'Never heard of dead marbles!' said the Reverend Cole.

'Not marbles,' said Jeremy James. 'Gerbils.'

'Ah!' said the Reverend Cole. 'Where are they?'

'Here,' said Jeremy James, holding out the liquorice allsort box.

'Thank you,' said the Reverend Cole. 'My favourite sweets.'

Getting the gerbils to heaven is only one of Jeremy James's problems. He also has to rescue Richard's gran from the lavatory, warn the fortune-teller about her future, and save the family from a life without chocolate.

The seventh book in the hilarious Jeremy James series.

David Henry Wilson titles available from Macmillan

The prices shown below are correct at the time of going to press. However, Macmillan Publishers reserve the right to show new retail prices on covers which may differ from those previously advertised.

DAVID HENRY WILSON

All Macmillan titles can be ordered at your local bookshop or are available by post from:

**Book Service by Post
PO Box 29, Douglas, Isle of Man IM99 1BQ**

Credit cards accepted. For details:
Telephone: 01624 675137
Fax: 01624 670923
E-mail: bookshop@enterprise.net

Free postage and packing in the UK.
Overseas customers: add £1 per book (paperback)
and £3 per book (hardback).